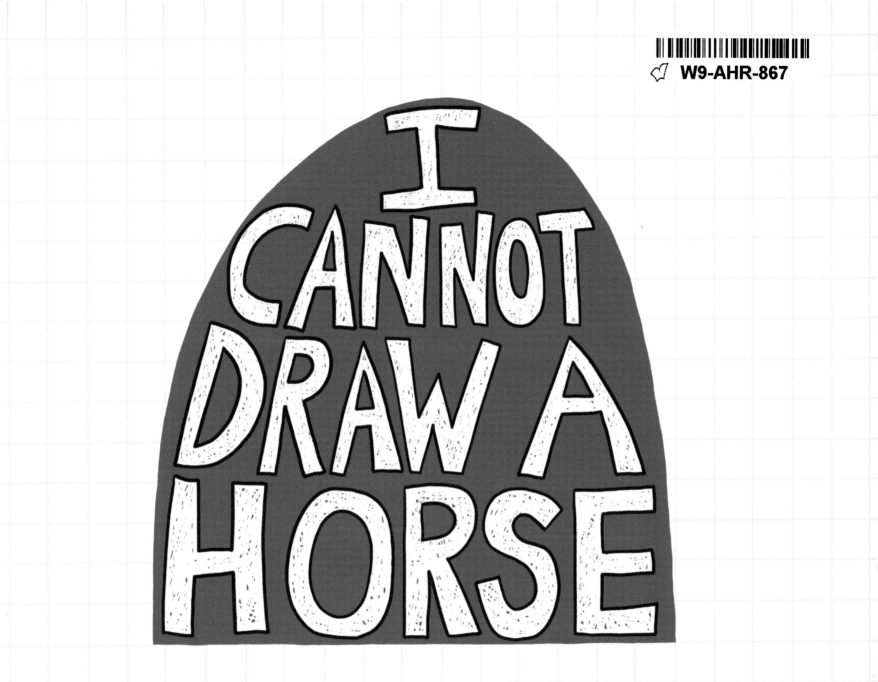

# I CANNOT DRAW A HORSE

## CHARISE MERICLE HARPER

union
square
kids

NEW YORK

This is my shape.

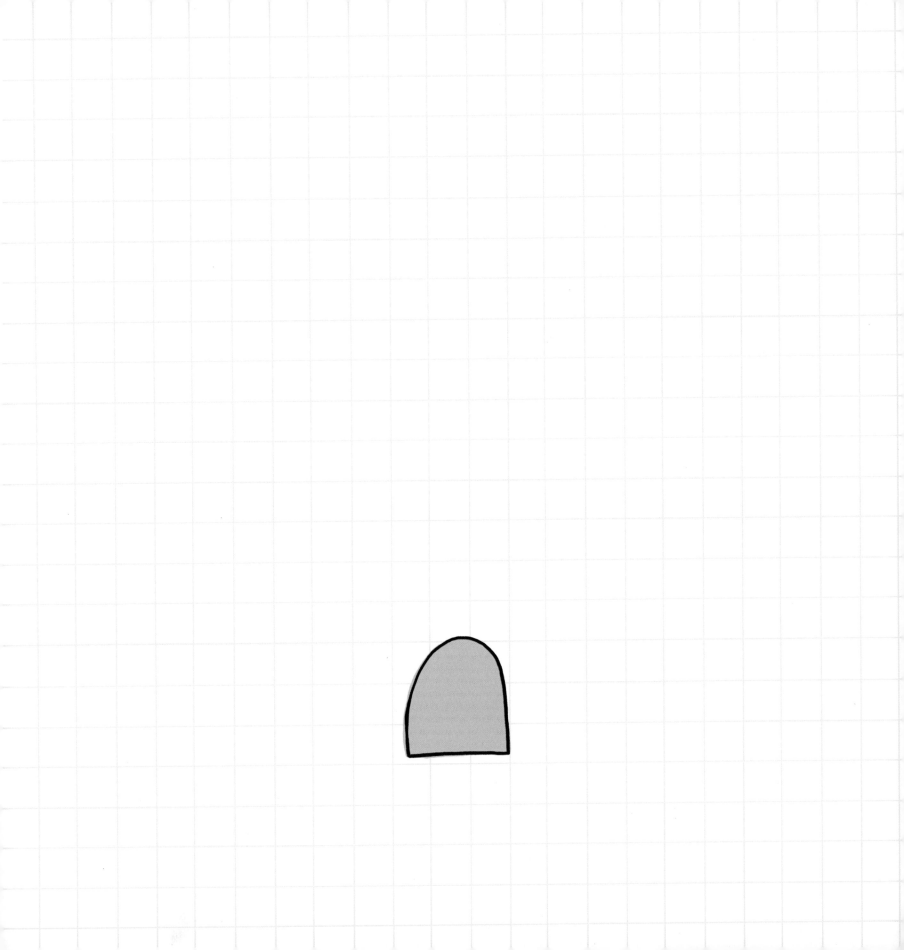

Hello, shape!

"What am I?" asked the shape.

You are not a nothing shape.

Look!

I can draw a cat.

A horse is hard to draw.
I cannot draw a horse.

BUT . . .

I can draw some friends.

I can draw . . .

a squirrel,               a beaver,               a bunny,

and a dog.

GRRR

That dog likes to jump and bark.

"That dog likes to jump and bark and RUN!" said the cat.

I can draw a hill.

I can draw a skateboard.

WHEEE!

Now you are safe.

"Safe is not fun," said the cat.

"I want some fun."

I cannot draw a horse.

BUT . . .

I can draw some fun.

I can draw a pool for splashing,

some rocks for jumping,

and an egg.

That egg can open.

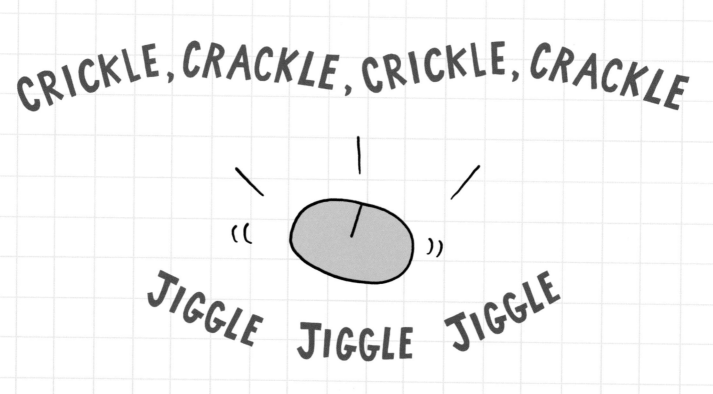

CRICKLE, CRACKLE, CRICKLE, CRACKLE

JIGGLE JIGGLE JIGGLE

"Who is inside?" asked the cat.

"That is not a horse," said the cat.

That turtle is slow.

"I want a fun, fast friend," cried the cat.

Did you say a house? I can draw a house.

"That is a big house," said the cat.

That house has a surprise.

"That is not a horse," said the cat.

That bear is very fast.

I can draw a ramp.

"Thank you," said the cat.

That cat is in trouble.

"SAVE ME!" yelled the cat.

I can draw a parachute.

I can draw some hay.

"I know who eats hay," said the cat.

Hay is good for rhyming!

Hay.

Day.

Clay.

I can draw some clay.

"Clay is good for play," said the cat.

A trophy is a special gift.
You must really believe in me.

I will try something new.

"Draw a horse!" cheered the cat.

LOOK!
I CAN draw a horse!

Here is your fun, fast friend.

"I do not want to run," said the horse.

A bicycle is hard to draw.
I cannot draw a bicycle.

**BUT** I can draw . . .